Ten Apples Up On Top!

By
Dr. Seuss*
*Writing as
Theo. LeSieg
Illustrated by
Roy McKie

Bright and Early Board Books™
RANDOM HOUSE NEW YORK

One apple
up on top!

Two apples
up on top!

Look, you.
I can do it, too.

Look!
See!
I can do three!

You can do three,
but I can do more.
You have three,
but I have four.

Look! See, now.
I can hop
with four apples
up on top.

And I can hop
up on a tree
with four apples
up on me.

Look here, you two.
See here, you two.
I can get five
on top.
Can you?

I am so good
I will not stop.
Five!
Now six!
Now seven on top!

Seven apples
up on top!
I am so good
they will not drop.

Five, six, seven!
Fun, fun, fun!
Seven, six, five,
four,
three,
two,
one!

But, see!
We are as good as you.
Look! Now we
have seven, too.

And now, see here.
Eight! Eight on top!

Eight apples up!
Not one will drop.

But I can do nine.
And hop!
And drink!
You can not do this,
I think.

Nine is very good.
But then . . .
Come on and we
will make it ten!

Look!

Ten

apples

up

on

top!

We are not

going to let them drop!

Classics made simpler and sturdier for the youngest readers!

Are You My Mother? by P. D. Eastman

Dr. Seuss's ABC by Dr. Seuss

The Foot Book by Dr. Seuss

Go, Dog. Go! by P. D. Eastman

Hand, Hand, Fingers, Thumb by Al Perkins

Inside, Outside, Upside Down by Stan & Jan Berenstain

Mr. Brown Can Moo! Can You? by Dr. Seuss

Old Hat, New Hat by Stan & Jan Berenstain

The Shape of Me and Other Stuff by Dr. Seuss

Stop, Train, Stop! by the Rev. W. Awdry

Ten Apples Up On Top! by Dr. Seuss

There's a Wocket in My Pocket! by Dr. Seuss

Random House
Seussville.com
randomhousekids.com
MANUFACTURED IN CHINA

Oh, the THINKS you Can Think!

by Dr. Seuss

A Bright and Early Board Book™
RANDOM HOUSE NEW YORK

You can think about red.
You can think about pink.
You can think up a horse.
Oh, the THINKS you can think!

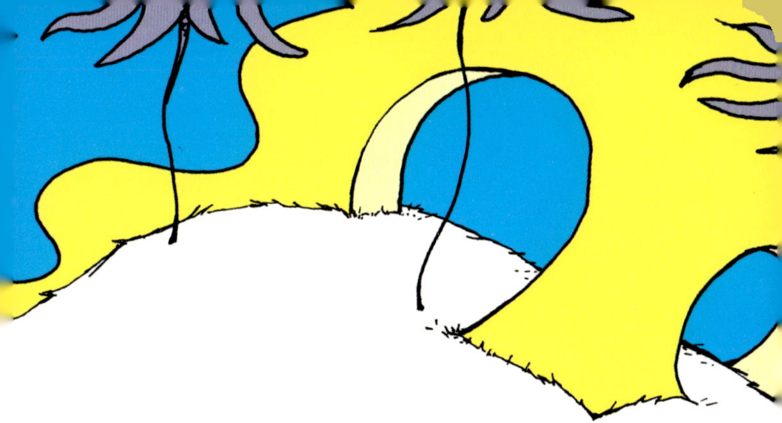

Oh, the THINKS
you can think up
if only you try!

If you try,
you can think up
a GUFF going by.

And you don't have to stop.
You can think about SCHLOPP.
Schlopp. Schlopp. Beautiful schlopp.
Beautiful schlopp
with a cherry on top.

You can think about Night,
a night in Na-Nupp.
The birds are asleep
and the three moons are up.

You can think about Day,
a day in Da-Dake.
The water is blue
and the birds are awake.

Think! Think and wonder.
Wonder and think.
How much water
can fifty-five elephants drink?

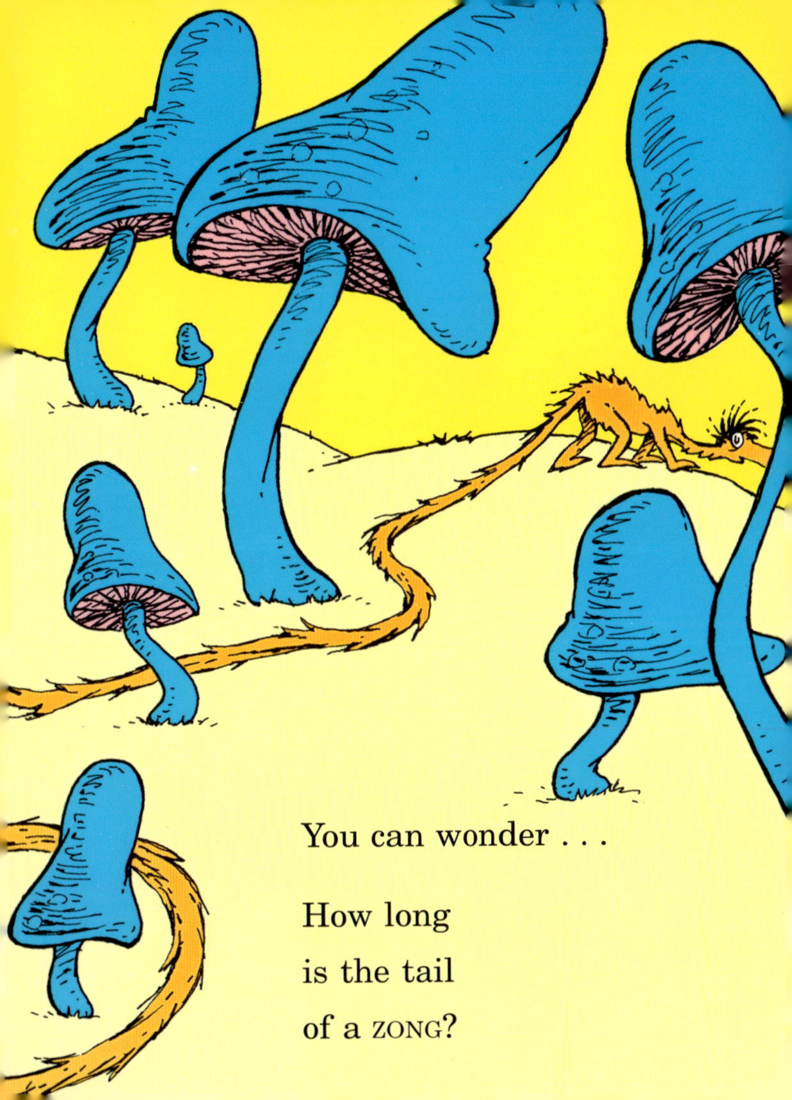

You can wonder . . .

How long
is the tail
of a ZONG?

Think of Light.
Think of Bright.
Think of
Stairs in the Night.

THINK!

Think a ship.

Think up a long trip.

Go visit the VIPPER,

the Vipper of Vipp.

Think left and think right
and think low and think high.
Oh, the THINKS you can think up if only you try!

Classics made simpler and sturdier for the youngest readers!

Are You My Mother? by P. D. Eastman
Dr. Seuss's ABC by Dr. Seuss
The Eye Book by Dr. Seuss
The Foot Book by Dr. Seuss
Go, Dog. Go! by P. D. Eastman
Hand, Hand, Fingers, Thumb by Al Perkins
He Bear, She Bear by Stan & Jan Berenstain
Hop on Pop by Dr. Seuss
Mr. Brown Can Moo! Can You? by Dr. Seuss
Old Hat, New Hat by Stan & Jan Berenstain
The Shape of Me and Other Stuff by Dr. Seuss
Ten Apples Up On Top! by Dr. Seuss
The Tooth Book by Dr. Seuss

Random House
Seussville.com
randomhousekids.com
MANUFACTURED IN CHINA

The SHAPE of ME and OTHER STUFF

Dr. Seuss's Surprising Word Book

Bright and Early Board Books™

RANDOM HOUSE NEW YORK

The shape of you

the
shape
of
me

the shape
of everything I see . . .

a bug...

a balloon

a bed

a bike.

No shapes are ever quite alike.

Just think about
the shape of beans

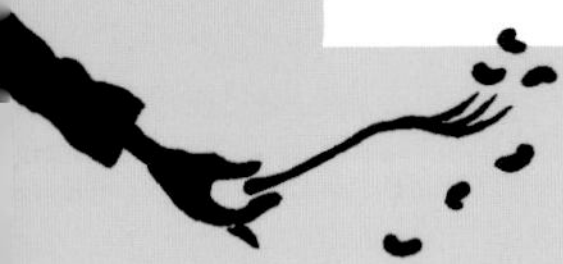

and flowers

and mice

and big machines!

Just think about
the shape of strings

and elephants.......................

..................and other things.

The shape of lips.

The shape of ships.

The shape
of water
when
it
drips.

And the shape of camels.........

....................the shape of bees

and the wonderful
shapes of back door keys!

And the shapes
of spider webs

and clothes!

And,

speaking of shapes,

now just suppose...!

Suppose
YOU
were shaped
like these...

...or those!

...or shaped
like a BLOGG!

Or a garden hose!

Of all
the shapes
we MIGHT have been...

I say, "HOORAY
for the shapes we're in!"

Classics made simpler and sturdier for the youngest readers!

Dr. Seuss's ABC by Dr. Seuss

The Foot Book by Dr. Seuss

Go, Dog. Go! by P. D. Eastman

Inside, Outside, Upside Down
by Stan & Jan Berenstain

Mr. Brown Can Moo! Can You?
by Dr. Seuss

Old Hat, New Hat
by Stan & Jan Berenstain

The Shape of Me and Other Stuff
by Dr. Seuss

There's a Wocket in My Pocket!
by Dr. Seuss

Random House
Seussville.com
randomhousekids.com
MANUFACTURED IN CHINA